Fraidy Cat

Caitlin,
May your fears
become your stepping
stones! Best wishes.
Melinda S Chambers
9/5/09

By Melinda Chambers

Illustrated by Sue Ann Maxwell Spiker

Fraidy Cat

by Melinda Chambers

Illustrated by Sue Ann Spiker

To order additional copies of this book
or for book publishing information, or to contact the author:

Headline Kids
P.O. Box 52
Terra Alta, WV 26764
www.headlinebooks.com

Tel/Fax: 800-570-5951
Email: mybook@headlinebooks.com

Headline Kids is an imprint of Headline Books

ISBN 0-929915-91-7
ISBN-13: 9780929915-91-3

Library of Congress Control Number: 2009929360

Grades K-6, Self Esteem, Character Enhancement

Chambers, Melinda
Fraidy Cat by Melinda Chambers,
Illustrations by Sue Ann Maxwell Spiker
Summary: Fraidy Cat learns not to be afraid to leave
the safety of his shelf in the barn by watching a mud
dauber build her nest.

[1. Cats-Fiction, 2. Wasps-Fiction]

PRINTED IN THE UNITED STATES OF AMERICA

Dedication

To those who have discovered that sometimes
you have to leap from the safety of your shelf to
get to where you need to be.

The sun peeped through the barn window as Mama Cat and her litter of young kittens began to stir. The kittens had just finished nursing and were eager to leave the shelf where they were born. This was the day when Mama Cat had promised them they could explore the large barn.

With Mama Cat's patient guidance, the kittens jumped down from the shelf. . .all of them, that is, except one little kitten.

"Meow. . .Meow. . .MEOW!"

"What's the matter? Are you hungry? Do you hurt? Are you cold?"

"No, I just want off this shelf so I can look around like the other kittens. . .but what if I land the wrong way or miss the spot I'm aiming for?"

"Well, that just might happen."

"Uh huh," responded the kitten. "That's just what I thought. That's why I'm not jumping."

"So, you're content to just watch from the shelf while your brothers and sisters explore the wonderful nooks and crannies of this big barn? You'll never find out what you can do if you don't take the first leap."

"But what if I get lost, or stuck, or. . ."

"ENOUGH! If you're such a FRAIDY CAT, I think you should just stay on that shelf until you're too big to fit on it. Of course, you'll miss out on all the great things there are to do and see around here."

"What do you mean?"

"Why, there's a great big world outside this barn that's just waiting for you and the other kittens to explore. But, of course, YOU'LL never know. . .that is, if you decide to stay on that shelf."

Fraidy Cat's siblings were having a great time playing in the big barn. They ran in circles trying to catch their tails and when they got tired of that, they played hide and seek among the hay bales and feed troughs. The cows and sheep who were boarding in the barn, and even the farmer who was milking the cows, were amused at their antics. The kittens didn't stop playing until nightfall, when they wearily made their way back to the safety of their shelf. There they joined Fraidy Cat.

"Why didn't you join us? We had so much fun today. . .and we got really good at jumping, and running, and climbing. We can hardly wait until tomorrow."

"Well, it didn't look like so much fun to me. I saw you bump your head on the feed trough and I saw you when you didn't know where everyone had gone, and. . ."

"Oh, sure, sometimes you have to take a chance. . .but if you don't TRY, you'll never find out what you can do."

"Yes, but you'll never fail, either."

"That's true, I guess. If you just spend your life on that shelf,you probably won't get hurt, or lost, or fail at something, but you'll also never find out what's on the other side of that barn door. Mama says tomorrow we're ready to go outside. We can hardly wait!"

The next morning came much too early as far as Fraidy Cat was concerned. Mama Cat and her kittens jumped off the shelf and were out the door, even before the rooster had crowed his wake-up call.

Fraidy Cat carefully looked around the barn. It was very quiet. Even the cows and sheep had gone outside the safety of the barn.

All that could be heard was the buzzing of a mud dauber in the webby rafters. With nothing better to do, Fraidy cleaned herself with her rough tongue and watched as the mud dauber slowly built a nest of mud.

The mud dauber would leave the safety of the barn, to return shortly carrying a tiny ball of mud with her forelegs. She would then carefully place the mud on the barn wall, molding it with her mouth parts and legs. When satisfied with the shape of the mud, she would once again fly outside the barn to repeat the cycle. Several times in the process the mud dauber would encounter obstacles, such as near misses with a cow's tail, but she never stopped making her nest.

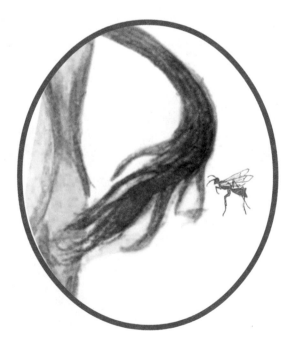

The nest was beginning to take shape with neat and orderly rows of mud. Growing weary of watching the numerous trips in and out of the barn, and listening to the gentle hum of the mud dauber's vibrating wings on her return trips, Fraidy Cat curled up in a ball and took a much needed nap in the safety of her shelf. When she awoke she was surprised to find that the mud dauber's nest had become a long cylinder and was now complete.

Slowly opening her eyes, Fraidy Cat watched in awe as the mud dauber then flew to the rafters in search of prey. Finding a spider, she would sting it to paralyze it. Once the spider could no longer move, the mud dauber stuffed it in her nest of mud. This process was repeated several times, as more and more spiders found their way inside her nest. When the nest was filled, she laid an egg on top of the spiders and then sealed the cylinder with more mud.

Completely occupied with the adventures of the mud dauber, Fraidy Cat hadn't noticed the return of his brothers and sisters until they jumped on the shelf next to him. "You should have been with us today. We saw birds, and grass, and trees, and ponds, and trucks, and above us we saw a great big blue sky. You'd never believe what a big place it is out there."

"I discovered that it was a pretty big place in the barn today, too," Fraidy Cat replied with equal enthusiasm, as the kittens snuggled close to Mama Cat and began nursing. Fraidy Cat had much to talk about and share with his siblings, but it could wait until dinner was over.

Sleep came much too soon for the weary kittens, but Fraidy Cat couldn't get the adventures of the mud dauber off his mind. For once he was looking forward to the next day to see if the mud dauber would return.

Sun beams began to peep through the cracks of the barn and once again it was morning. "Hey, Fraidy, why don't you come with us?" the kittens asked as they skillfully jumped from the shelf.

"No, I'm just not ready to go, yet," Fraidy Cat answered, with a bit of anxiety in his voice.

Mama Cat just shook her head as she led the other kittens out the barn door.

Fraidy Cat listened quietly for the return of the mud dauber. Not to be disappointed, it wasn't long before she heard the familiar buzzing sounds entering the barn door. The mud dauber wasted no time as she began her rounds of bringing more mud to her nest. Today, however, she started a new nest beside the other one. Trip after trip was made, carrying a small ball of mud and shaping it into a perfect little cylinder.

Taking a short nap, Fraidy Cat was awakened by the sound of buzzing. Opening his eyes, he was startled to find the mud dauber dancing in the air right in front of him with her legs dangling in space. Eye ball to eye ball it was as if the mud dauber was asking him why he was just sitting there.

Fraidy Cat could think of all kinds of reasons why he hadn't moved from the shelf, but none of them seemed very good at that moment. In fact, he couldn't resist the urge to make the first leap. Gathering all of his strength and courage, he held his breath as he plopped from the shelf.

When he took another breath he was surprised to find that he was on the barn floor. "Well, that wasn't so bad," he thought. In fact, he wondered why he hadn't done it sooner.

Days passed quickly in the lives of the kittens, who were now growing by leaps and bounds. The shelf where they were born looked much smaller, and its safety was no longer needed. The mud dauber's nest continued to grow. It now had five more cylinders. But, the biggest change had occurred with Fraidy Cat.

During the process of watching the mud dauber patiently building her rows of nests, Fraidy realized for himself that he could never get somewhere by going nowhere. The shelf was nice and safe, but offered nothing else.

Fraidy now answers to a different name. With the wisdom he gained through his daily observations and his cautious nature, Fraidy has become quite a respected leader among the cat family and now proudly answers to TOP CAT.

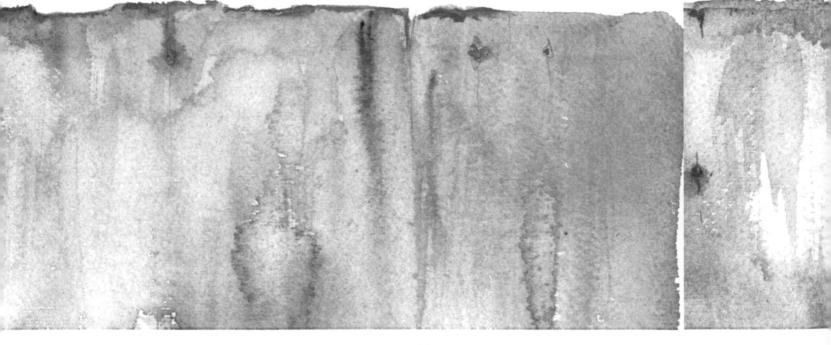

Organ-pipe Mud Dauber
Wasps
Order: Hymenoptera
Family: Sphecidae
Genus and species:
Trypoxylon politum

The organ-pipe mud dauber is a common wasp whose home is recognized more often that the insect itself. It is about an inch long and bluish-black, with a very thin waist. Mud daubers are solitary wasps that construct small nests of mud in or around homes, sheds, and barns and under open structures, bridges and similar sites. This wasp group is named for the nests that are made from the mud collected by the females. The organ-pipe mud dauber builds cylindrical tubes resembling pipe-organ pipes.

Mud is rolled into a ball, carried to the nest, and molded into place with the wasp's mandibles. The female forms a strip of mud for the tubular nest with each load, alternating from one side to the other. Nest construction is often accompanied by bursts of buzzing that are amplified by the hallow nest, producing a "singing-like" sound. A typical pipe contains 3 to 4 cells, and a typical nest includes a cluster of 5 to 7 pipes.

After completing the mud nest, the female captures several insects or spiders to place in the cells. Prey are stung and paralyzed before being placed in the nest. A single egg is deposited on the prey within each cell, and the cell is then sealed with mud. During this whole process, the male mud daubers guard the nest from intruders. Once the nest is completed the adult mud daubers leave.

The larvae that hatch from the eggs feed on the prey items left by the adult wasp. When the larvae are done growing, they spin cocoons and change into the pupa stage. Each new insect spends the winter as a pupa and emerges as an adult mud dauber early the next summer. Once the adult mud dauber has left its cocoon, it must chew through the wall of its tube. Now the mud dauber can look for a mate and start the cycle over again.

Solitary wasps, such as the mud daubers, do not defend their nest the way social wasps such as hornets and yellowjackets do. Mud daubers are very unlikely to sting unless they are seriously provoked.

Mud daubers pose little threat, and should be regarded as beneficial insects since they remove and use as prey many species of spiders. The mud nests can be scraped off and discarded if they are objectionable.